W9-AXP-540

INDIANA JONES

AND THE
SPEAR OF DESTINY

PART THREE

SCRIPT & COLORS
Elaine Lee

ART
Dan Spiegle

LETTERS
Carrie Spiegle

COVER ART
Hugh Fleming

DARK HORSE COMICS

Spotlight

VISIT US AT
www.abdopublishing.com

Library of Congress Cataloging-in-Publication Data

Lee, Elaine.
  Indiana Jones and the Spear of Destiny / Elaine Lee, script, colors ; Will Simpson, pencils ; Dan Spiegle, inks ; Clem Robins, letters ; Hugh Fleming, cover art ; Teena Gores, publication design ; Bob Cooper & Dan Thorsland, edits. -- Reinforced library bound ed.
      p. cm. -- (Indiana Jones)
  "Dark Horse."
  ISBN 978-1-59961-579-0 (vol. 3)
  1. Graphic novels. [1. Graphic novels.] I. Simpson, Will, ill. II. Title.
PZ7.7.L44In 2008
[Fic]--dc22
                                        2008009794

All Spotlight books have reinforced library bindings and are manufactured in the United States of America.

AS I WAS SAYING, REBECCA, THE HILL WAS CALLED GORSEDD ARBETH AND, SHOULD A MAN OF ROYAL BLOOD SPEND A NIGHT UPON IT, HE WOULD EITHER RECEIVE WOUNDS AND BLOWS OR SEE A MARVEL.

TAKE ME TO IT THEN! I'M SURE TO SEE A WONDER! DID I MENTION, REBECCA, ABOUT MY BEIN' A DIRECT DESCENDANT OF NIAL OF THE NINE HOSTAGES?

I BELIEVE YOU DID, BRENDAN.

AS I RECALL, MR. O'NEAL, YOU SLID IT IN SOMEWHERE BETWEEN THE LIST OF YOUR ADMIRABLE QUALITIES AND THE TRIBUTE TO BRIAN BORU.

THE NOBLE PROGENITOR OF THE O'BRIAN CLAN AND M' MOTHER'S OWN TRIBE!

NOW, WE NEED ONLY ACQUIRE THE *HEARTWOOD* OF THE HOLY *THORN* SO THAT WE MAY RE-CREATE THE *SHAFT* OF THE SPEAR. YOU MAY *HIT* HIM NOW.

FOLLOW ME!

UNGH!

YOUR IRISH FRIEND HAS FLED IN A MOST COWARDLY FASHION. HE WILL BE HELP TO YOU. BUT THE WATER IS BEAUTIFUL IN THE MOONLIGHT, IS IT NOT? TIE HIM, KURT.

DO YOU THINK THE REICH A CAMELOT, YOUNG SEIG? WOULD YOU HELP THESE MEN TURN THE WORLD TO A WASTELAND?

I SUGGEST YOU MAKE PEACE WITH YOUR OWN SON, DR. JONES, AND LEAVE MINE TO ME. THE STONE, NOW, KURT.

WE HAVE DECIDED TO *KEEP* YOUR FATHER WITH US. HE IS A SOURCE OF INFORMATION THAT MAY PROVE *USEFUL* TO US. ALSO, MISS STEIN...

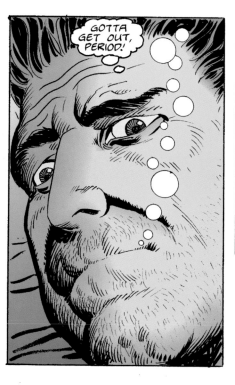

KER-ACK PLOW KER-ACK-PLOW KER-ACK PLOW

QUIET, NOW, THEY'RE HARDLY DOWN THE CREST 'O THE HILL!

THAT'LL BE OUR *TIRES* THEY'RE SHOOTIN' OUT. WE'RE SURELY DOOMED.

LOATHSOME FASCISTS! AND THEY CALLED *ME* A COWARD, AND THEM HIDING BEHIND A WOMAN AND AN OLD MAN! THEY'LL BE HEADING FOR THE *FERRY* AT *HOLYHEAD*, LITTLE GOOD THE KNOWING WILL *DO* US! WE'RE ABANDONED!

GRIM, STARK, AND DESOLATE! LIKE THE PLAIN OF ILL-LUCK THE HERO OF ULSTER WAS FORCED TO CROSS, AND US WITHOUT AN APPLE AND WHEEL!

SHUT UP, O'NEAL! WE'LL FIND WHEELS. THIS IS SHEEP COUNTRY. WHERE THERE'RE SHEEP, THERE'RE SHEPHERDS AND WHERE THERE'RE SHEPHERDS, WE'LL FIND WHEELS.

HOPE THEY AREN'T ATTACHED TO ANOTHER HORSE CART!

QUICKLY, YOU IDIOTS! FIND IT, QUICKLY!

REBECCA!

UNGH!

GO, DR. JONES...NOW!

IT'S A LOVELY EVENIN' FOR A SWIM, SIR...

...AND ONLY A WEE BIT COLDER THAN SNOW ON A GRAVESTONE.

O'NEAL? SHUT UP.

OVER HERE!

LATER...

TOO BAD THE FASCISTS WISED UP AND DECIDED TO WRAP THE TWO HALVES OF THE SPEAR POINT SEPARATELY!

I HATE THAT WE LOST *REBECCA*!

WE'LL FIND HER, SON.

RIGHT AND TRUE! BUT, THAT WAS *STILL* A GRAND IDEA I HAD, IF YOU DON'T MIND ME *SAYIN'* SO... SWITCHIN' THE SPEARS AND ALL.

IDEA *YOU* HAD! WHO DO YOU THINK *GAVE* YOU THE OTHER SPEAR, ANY-WAY? I HATE THAT I *LOST* THAT THING, TOO!

WIND'S PICKING UP! MIGHT BE A STORM COMIN'!

GOOD LORD, WHAT'S THAT?!

HOLY SMOKE! A *SNORKEL!* I HEARD THE GERMANS WERE USING 'EM ON THEIR SUBS! LETS 'EM STAY OUT A LOT LONGER WITHOUT HAVING TO SURFACE...RADAR CAN'T PICK 'EM UP!

YOU THINK THEY'RE LOOKING FOR US?

IF THEY WERE, WE'D ALREADY BE DEAD.

IT'S MOVING AWAY QUITE FAST!

YEAH, THEY *DO* THAT, DAD. BETTER GET THE SAIL DOWN. THIS WIND'S STARTING TO FEEL *DANGEROUS!*

WE SPLIT UP HERE.

NO! NO! YOU'LL NOT BE GETTIN' RID O' ME NOW. YOU'LL BE NEEDIN' MY HELP WITH THOSE BAD, BAD BOYS!

I NEED YOU TO STAY WITH THE SPEAR. I DON'T WANT TO LOSE IT AGAIN. TAKE IT TO NEW GRANGE. FIND COVER AND WAIT FOR ME THERE.

I KNOW THE WAY. I'LL GET US THERE SAFELY, YOU CAN BE SURE!

WHERE ARE YOU GOING, JUNIOR?

BACK TO CONNELY'S PLACE. TO GET REBECCA AND THE OTHER HALF OF THE SPEAR.

WON'T THEY BE EXPECTING YOU?

THEY CERTAINLY WILL.